D1571620

Paperback ISBN: 979-8-9871171-3-2

Hardcover ISBN: 979-8-9871171-4-9

Ebook ISBN: 979-8-9871171-5-6

Library of Congress Number: 2023907921

Edited by: Two Tales Editing, LLC

For more information or to purchase signed, dedicated copies visit:
www.kristinasheldonauthor.com

Kristina Sheldon
CHILDREN'S AUTHOR

INSPIRED BY MOTHERHOOD

This book belongs to:

_____

For my wildflower, my little girl.

To the strong women who have raised me.
Thank you for encouraging my
strength and independence.
I am the mother I am today
because of each of you.

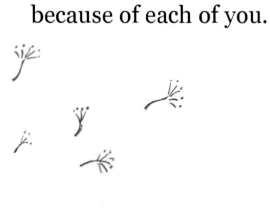

Wandering through fields,
smiling, laughing, picking flowers.
My darling, spunky, little girl,
these are your super powers.

Wild like a dandelion,
swaying in the wind.
You are happy and free-spirited,
on that I can depend.

Sweet as honeysuckle,
whose sweet scent fills the air.
Picking, weaving buttercups—
a crown of flowers for your hair.

Shining bright like a sunflower,
basking brilliantly in the sun.
You radiate joy and wonder,
and you make life oh so fun.

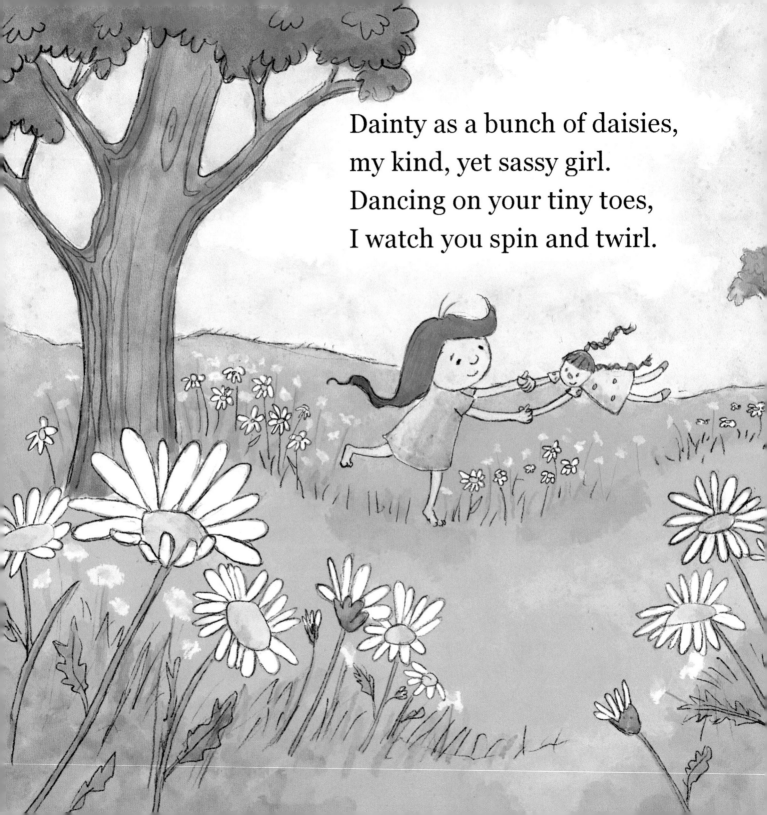

Dainty as a bunch of daisies,
my kind, yet sassy girl.
Dancing on your tiny toes,
I watch you spin and twirl.

Strong like an oak tree,
so mighty, great, and tall.
Steady through all seasons,
you catch leaves as they fall.

Singing proudly like the songbirds,
as they go flying through the air.
Watch as each lands in a tree,
no other bird-song can compare.

Bubbly like a roaring creek,
water running fast and cold.

Jumping, skipping, rock to rock,
you are agile, swift, and bold.

Friendly as a ladybug,
making friends on every trail.
Stopping to smell the violets,
you smile with each inhale.

Busy as a bumblebee,
humming, buzzing, speeding 'round.
Your laughter fills our adventures
with my most favorite sound.

Colorful as the setting sky,
hues of orange, purple, and pink.
Dazzling in the golden glow,
you care not what others think.

Sparkling like a field of fireflies,
lighting up a darkening sky.
You fill your jar, one by one,
in amazement as they pass by.

Of all the pretty birds and flowers,
bumblebees, and ladybugs,
my favorite thing by far, sweet girl,
is sharing big bear hugs.

I'll hold you as you grow, and
like blooming petals that uncurl,
there is no one as unique as you,
my wildflower, my little girl.

About the Author

Kristina Sheldon is a wife, mother, nurse, and author from Chesterfield, Virginia. Inspired by motherhood, Kristina's first book, *My Very First Friend*, reminisces on the milestones that babies meet with their furry best friend at their side. Now, Kristina dedicates a love letter to her daughter. *My Wildflower* is a rhyming picture book that describes a closeness to nature to highlight her daugher's tenacity and spirit.

Kristina fiercely believes that she comes from a line of women who instilled the values of strength, determination, and independence into their children. If not for the women before her, Kristina would not be the mother she is today. She looks forward to raising children to believe in themselves and to chase their dreams, whatever they may be.

To learn more about Kristina and her books, visit:
www.kristinasheldonauthor.com

Kristina Sheldon
CHILDREN'S AUTHOR

INSPIRED BY MOTHERHOOD

More from the Author

Were you a dog mom before becoming a human mom?

Introducing our babies to our fur babies is an exciting time as parents!

From coming home from the hospital to the first day of school,
My Very First Friend explores the milestones our babies meet with their
furry best friends at their side. Like many millennial families, Kristina
was a parent to her fur babies first. As new parents, we joyfully watch
our fur babies and human babies develop a special and unique bond.
My Very First Friend captures the bittersweet feeling of watching our
dogs age as our families begin.

Made in the USA
Las Vegas, NV
15 April 2024

88727083R00017